D1484071

This book is dedicated to all Astros fans:

the young, the young at heart, and

everyone in between.

www.mascotbooks.com

Orbit's First Day of School

©2017 Houston Astros, LLC. All Rights Reserved. No part of this
publication may be reproduced, stored in a retrieval system or transmitted
in any form by any means electronic, mechanical, or photocopying,
recording or otherwise without the permission of the Houston Astros.

All Houston Astros indicia are protected trademarks or registered
trademarks of the Houston Astros and are used under license.

For more information, please contact:
Mascot Books
620 Herndon Parkway #320
Herndon, VA 20170
info@mascotbooks.com

CPSIA Code: PRT1117A
ISBN-13: 978-1-68401-227-5

Printed in the United States

ORBIT'S
FIRST DAY OF SCHOOL

KYLE HAMSHER

illustrated by Brian Martin

ORBIT is an alien from outer space and the official team mascot of the Houston Astros baseball team!

Before Orbit came to Earth to cheer on the Astros, he lived in a special place in outer space called the Grand Slam Galaxy, where he excelled in all sorts of activities such as moonwalking, crater-jumping, and of course, baseball!

ORBIT ALWAYS MADE SURE TO PUT HIS STUDIES FIRST.

He knew that before he could do any of his favorite activities, like playing baseball, he had to get all of his homework done and make good grades in school.

After landing on Earth and making the city of Houston his home, Orbit realized that his education would be even more important, which meant he had to stay in school – especially because he had all sorts of new things to learn about life on Earth!

ORBIT WENT TO THE LOCAL SCHOOL

and met the principal. She was very nice and a big fan of the Astros! She told Orbit about all the great things he would learn. Orbit got very excited about his new school!

THE NEXT MORNING, Orbit ate a good, healthy breakfast before heading out to the bus stop where he met some kids from his neighborhood who rode the same bus.

The bus ride to school was really fun for Orbit – it was his first time to ever ride a bus! In the Grand Slam Galaxy, everyone travelled by spaceship, cosmo-cab, and hover board. Orbit liked how the bus driver drove that big bus!

WHEN ORBIT GOT TO SCHOOL,

he walked into his classroom where he met his new teacher and classmates.

As Orbit made his way to his desk, he started to get a little nervous. Everybody was looking at him, and he realized that he didn't know anybody in his classroom. He started to get a little bit scared because he was in a brand-new place.

WHEN ORBIT GOT TO HIS DESK, the boy sitting next to him introduced himself.

"Hi!" he said. "My name is Richard! I was a new student last year, so I know how scary it can be to come to a new place where you don't know anyone. Don't worry, though, you can hang out with me and I'll introduce you to some of my friends when we go out for recess!"

This made Orbit feel better.

ORBIT WAS EXCITED ABOUT RECESS!

He followed Richard and the rest of his class outside where everyone was running, playing, and having a lot of fun! Orbit was very excited to join in!

RICHARD TOLD ORBIT that he could play basketball with him and some other kids. Orbit had never played basketball, so he wasn't very good. Some of the kids began to laugh at him.

"LET'S TRY A GAME OF TAG!"

said Richard. Orbit wasn't very good at tag either, because he was much bigger than the other kids and kept getting tagged out.

JUST THEN, some kids from another classroom started laughing at Orbit because he looked different. They started making fun of him for having green fur and a big belly. These kids were bullies – and Orbit didn't know what to do because he had never been bullied in the Grand Slam Galaxy.

Richard saw what was happening and ran over to a teacher for help. He explained that Orbit was being picked on for being different. The teacher knew exactly what to do.

GYMNA

AFTER RECESS,
it was time for PE. Orbit began to get nervous again because he knew those bullies from recess would be there, too. After being made fun of for not being good at basketball or tag, PE was the last place Orbit wanted to be. Orbit was beginning to get homesick and missed his friends back in the Grand Slam Galaxy.

WHEN EVERYONE GOT TO THE GYM,

Orbit saw a familiar sight! The PE teacher was standing in the middle of the room with a baseball in one hand and a bat in the other. Today they would be playing baseball – Orbit's favorite sport!

The PE teacher asked if anyone had ever played baseball before, and Orbit's hand shot straight up!

"Hey! I know who you are," said the PE teacher. "You're Orbit! You're the mascot for the Houston Astros!" Everyone looked at Orbit again, but this time, they were smiling! The PE teacher asked Orbit, "Will you please help me show everyone how to play baseball?"

ORBIT ENTHUSIASTICALLY AGREED!

He was so excited and spent the rest of the class time showing everyone how to hit, catch, and throw. He had the best time and made a lot of new friends!

After PE, some of the kids who picked on Orbit came up to him and apologized for being mean. They were very impressed with how good Orbit was at baseball and asked if he could show them more after school! They asked if they could be friends and learned to respect Orbit for who he was, not what he looked like.

When Orbit got home from school, he was so excited to tell his friends back in the Grand Slam Galaxy about his first day of school – how he rode a bus for the first time, learned new things, and even made some new friends by showing them how good he was at baseball…

BUT NOT UNTIL HE FINISHED HIS HOMEWORK!

TALKING POINTS
FOR ADULTS

Being in a new place

What were some of the hard moments Orbit faced on his first day of school? Have you ever felt any of the same things Orbit felt?

Richard offering friendship

Making new friends, especially in a new place, isn't always easy. It certainly wasn't easy for Orbit! How do you make new friends? Why do you think it's important to make new people feel welcome, just like Richard did?

Embracing our differences

When the bullies were making fun of Orbit for looking different than the rest of the kids, how do you think that made him feel? How do you think the other kids at school should have treated Orbit, as someone who looked different and came from a different place? How would you have treated Orbit?

Telling an adult about bullying

When Orbit was being bullied, why was it important that Richard told the teacher what was happening? Have you seen other kids get bullied? What would you do or say to help them?

Celebrating our strengths

Orbit wasn't very good at some of the activities the other children were playing, such as basketball and tag, but he was VERY good at baseball! What are some activities you are good at?

Practicing respect

Why is it important that we respect one another and treat each other with kindness? How do you practice respect with your parents, teachers, and friends?

THIS BOOK IS MADE POSSIBLE THROUGH THE GENEROUS SUPPORT OF PHILLIPS 66!

A proud sponsor of the Houston Astros, Phillips 66 is committed to the people of Houston, which is why they invest in education, literacy, community safety, emergency preparedness, the environment, and sustainability.

Phillips 66 is also the proud sponsor of Orbit's Reading Rally school assembly program, which educates students on the importance of reading, as well as the Astros Foundation Literacy Bus, which brings books to HISD schools and students.

For more information, please visit www.astros.com/orbit.

CAN YOU SPOT THE DIFFERENCES?

There are ten differences in the picture below.
Can you find them all?

ORBIT APPEARANCES AND EDUCATIONAL SCHOOL SHOWS

Book Orbit for your next event! He does birthday parties, corporate events, charity functions, and more!

Orbit also offers a complete line of educational assembly shows that cover topics such as literacy, anti-bullying, STEM, and making smart decisions such as saying no to drugs.

For more information, please call 713-259-8303 or visit www.astros.com/orbit.

You can also find Orbit on Facebook and Twitter

 /ORBITASTROS

 @ORBITASTROS

5